I0829502

This book has no AI images or writing

THIS BOOK BELONGS TO:

FAIRY LIGHTS

Bed Time Poems
& Gallery of Fairytale Art from Yesteryear

BY

HELEN WILLIFORD-LOWER

Within are many stories passed down among the Fae now told
to you for retelling. From Nordic, Irish and Greek legend to
New World myth - meet nature spirits, shape shifters,
hauntings, undersea creatures, elven blood, enchanting fairies
and their Royals, elemental landscapes and feisty animal
souls- all forming the luminous bedtime world of Fairy Lights.

Published April 9, 2025
© Helen Williford-Lower
Fabled Pen Press
Flaxmere, New Zealand
ISBN# 9780473742454
Book and Cover Design by Helen W-L

Dedicated To :

Titiana
Gloriana
Clair de Lune
Queene Brigid Danae and Saint Brigid
In All Her Forms and Fascinations

As well As Every Child and Inner Child

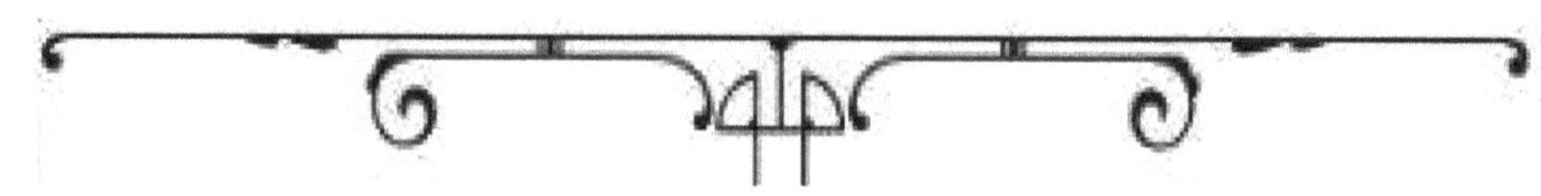

CONTENTS

~Spring~

~Summer~

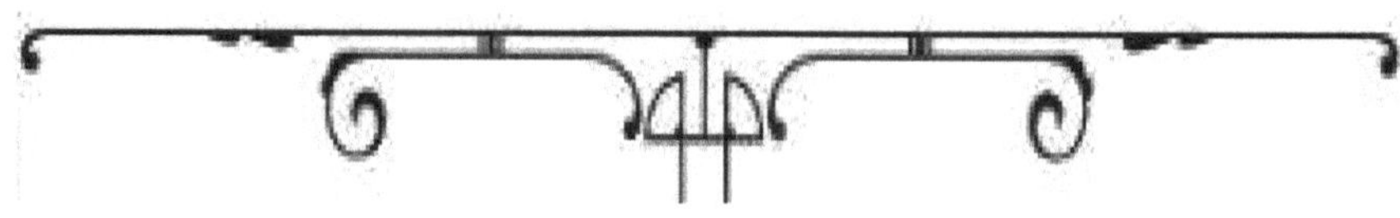

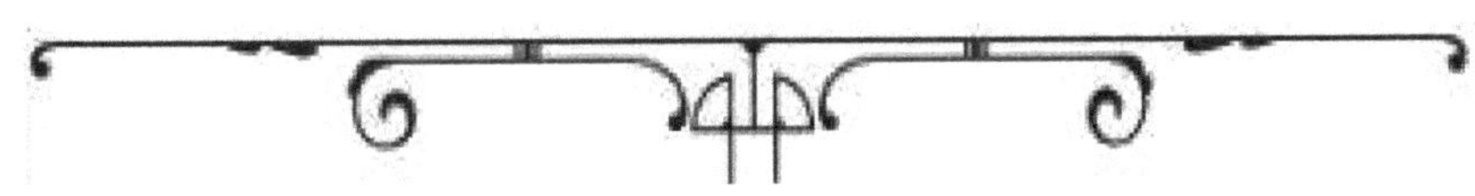

CONTENTS

~Autumn~

Vanishing Muse
Invocation of Fall
Rarebit
To Wee Russet Tuft
Onyx
The Spice Box

~Winter~

Dreamtime
Helland
Spirit of the Windward Isle
The Baallad of Blaackie Coal
The Dream Fairy
Far Rockaway

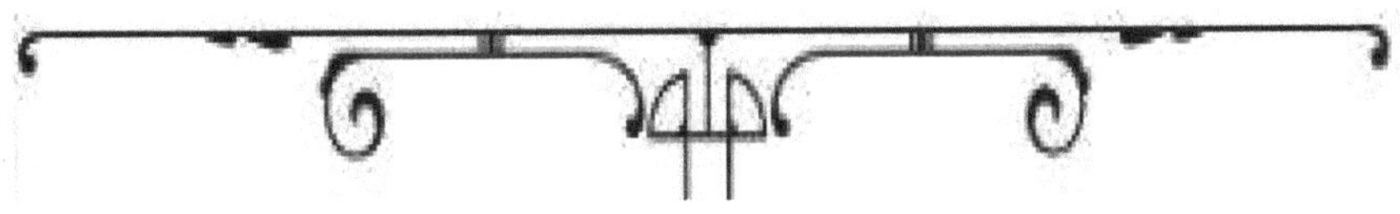

9

SPRING

Night's storms departed and dawn is risen,
The sun will gloriously rise;
Awake, Awake, to a new day's vision,
Reflecting in new opened eyes!

Timegarden

Beneath the bursting berry hedges,
A garden lined in thyme edges
Past the Poppies of pure wonder;
The stilling setting sun is all asunder

Silver pears and Apples d'Or
Embroidering petals on a sylvan floor
Shivering legions of poppies in wonder;
Over mirrored lakes the sun sets under

Saffron crocus scents lavender skies,
Golden red honey runs wild in sighs
Dripping on poppies of pure wonder;
Drenching the setting sun's still thunder

St. Paddy's Fete

There are sticks and twiggy things

Fine made faces and lace-like wings

Gold-rosy twilight, end of day -

Glamouring moonrise of the fae...

Rabbit's whiskers and horns so pluckie

Tinkle bell toes flit o'er the muckie -

Ghosty wee-folk, lit from within

Rumble tumble come the djinn!

Faery dust on wings with eyes

Flutter butter wayward cries --

Beneath an arching grassy knoll

Shining Folk parade and stroll...

Popping seedpods wake the Queenie,

All the company in tip-top greenie

Flower hair cups and curling boots

Brownies strike up acorn flutes!

Margaret W. Tarrant

Nectar beer and honey
plunder

Dancing motes gasp in
wonder...

Invisible, subtle, vapors
on air,

Children alone can see
them there.

All night 'neath
sylvan
moonset

Lasts the circling
fairy fete...

Each will have their
chance to say,

To sing, to eat,
perform and sashay,

THE LANTERN DANCE

To fly, to leap and flash about,

To listen in delight and

then to shout,

In silvery voices, light

and keen,

Paying grace to King

and Queene…

Who royally bestow their kiss,

"Goodeve my bonnies", "Now sleep in bliss!"

And with natural magic fed

They'll seek a favorite fairy bed --

Nut, shut flower or curled leaf is fine,

Spiderweb pillow and a drop o'dew wine.

After revels, what do fairies do?

They dream for hours - imagining YOU.

A Piece of Amber

Fair Amberglade and dark Mothstone

Walked together when they didn't walk alone,

Down the fruited paths of the forest shade

And that was how their love was made.

Through the misty sprays of the winding dell

The songs of Amberglade softly fell

On the ears of the green forest folk…

...And it was a song of love she spoke.

Under the ivy leaves of the dripping dell

Mothstone cast his moonlight spell

In circles of stars and night's deeper shade

He spoke to the heavens of Amberglade.

The spring runs lightly under sylvan shade

and more lightly still is fairy love made

so rare 'twas that such a legend was born

'twixt the setting sun and the white moon's horn ~

He vowed, "I will take my last breath."

She vowed, "I will weep myself to death"

He said, "Wrap your honey arms round me dear and I will forever keep your company here

Under the spider webs and early flowers

Near the tree roots where we spent our favorite hours…"

"But your wings will no longer catch the moon,"
she sighed

"Nor your honey voice golden the afternoon,"
he replied

"Nor your jet eyes blacken the night,"

"Nor your halo hair hold the sunlight."

And knowing this was true Amberglade
wept and cried

Near the tree roots where each the other
first spied

Here it was that Amberglade
wept and cried

Golden tears over Mothstone,
who happily died.

The centuries passed, and the fairy folk
did hide

While human children played near the tree
and spied

A Perfect Golden Amber Dome

Where a black moth made his eternal home -

Never to lose the touch of his love,

Nor her to ever lose his powers from above.

The spring runs lightly under sylvan shade

and more lightly still is fairy love made,

So rare 'twas such a legend was born

'twixt the setting sun and the white moon's horn ~

That now when a rare fairy marriage is sworn

In a circle of night dew
before early morn,

The greenfolk invoke the love

that does not fade

Between dark Mothstone
and his fair Amberglade.

The Redeemables

On a still hill like a

sunrise it seems

the fire of The Lady

in each holy spring

gleams,

Through dim

memories of

airy dreams,

Her shiny troops

gliding along --

To sing of it once more in song!

How this daydreamer came to be

Poetess Queene of all Faerie

Is stuff of most fanciful inquiry,

Her dragonflies bronzing along --

    To sing of it once more in song!

Hi! Among the stream stone hops,

Ho! Trooping along tree tops,

Riding side-saddle on poppy mops

Pale friends dancing along --

　　To sing of it once more in song!

So on Easter day-morn it seems

New dew in springtide redeems

Each madcap

season of faery

scenes,

Her shining

troops lolloping

on--

　　To sing of it

once more in

song!

The pearly dewborn reverie fades

Notorious night-deeds of fairydust days

Falling away in sheer cascades-

Her pale ones home-hoofing along --

To sing of it once more in song!

My Monumental Teeth

Time worn altars
in the church of my
incense mouth,
My oracle's bones
are ivory and white
casting shadows like a
still life marbleized
meditative sight…
While pale gold
accretions of a few
lifetime nights
of living poetry
stalactites form under
the full moon's salty white secretions…

Over an eternal reliquary,

A stony tomb,

An open air sanctuary

perfumed;

Where small sprites trespass and listen

for the magic there, and trace a jewel

in the still scented sparkling air,

Where no birds wings whir over statues of

fabulous fossilized pearly

wealth, whereTime itself

now enters reverently to order

the spell which compels

the senses to sleep…

under that luminescent reef

which glistens in the secret

lair of my monumental teeth.

35

SUMMER

The mountain white, the sapphire sky,
The lily moon, the stars on high,
The mellow laughing loving sun,
And All is said, and All is done.

ONE BRIGHT SUMMER'S NIGHT A NUMBER OF FAERIES FLEW

INTO THE ROOM

My Waikouaiti Lass

'n her wild southern graces…

I didnae love the land enough,

yet somehow she loved me;

Her pastel cliffs tumbled down

to the blue southern sea,

All the boon she offered me,

she offered me for free -

I weren't half-good enough, to a love such as she.

She offered me isolation, splendid and fine

'Neath my cottage door's pink petaling vine -

Her black oak limbs netted the winter starshine,

In spring, the bees shared wi' me

her wild plum wine.

Her changin' moods were those
of a dancin' elfin child -
Some sunshine smiles -- then storm winds
breakin' wild!
Leaping lambs ramblin' on emerald paddocks styled
Rustic, like a story in a faeryland beguiled.

I tried tae love her hillocks, but she loved me more -
Gave me gold sparklin' sand
and a vast secluded shore,
Gave me brilliant singin' birds and
all the gems they wore,
And ever' night her lullaby
was the rhymin' ocean roar.

Her splendid isolation for a spell was all o' mine;
Her purple thistle's bristle and blush clematis vine,
Her blooming elderberry and beach fringed wi' pine,
Her fresh cold airs were draughts of southern wine.

It's nae like th' daffodils don't gleam in ither places,
It's nae like thar's no nicer folks wi' friendlier faces,
But th' warm weather cities 'n' their trappin' rat races
Canna' surpass mah Waikouait' lass 'n' her
wild southern graces.

I've left her now, but in my heart, I can surely see
Her tussock grass and yellow broom waving merrily,
All the boon she offered me, she offered me for free -
I didnae love her half-enough,
yet she still loves me.

The Elder Tree

Come on a shaft of starlit morn;

Taking me under the Elder tree -

It was in the branch, the berry and the thorn,

He made himself well-known to me.

Coat, young sun-like; boots, leaves of green,

I'm blind now, and why I canna say -

But gazing in the eyes of the Elven King

The weary-world realm can slip away…

ZÉLIE AND THE FAIRY CANDIDE "PRINCE CHÉRI"

Dawn always comes, a-clinging

    I've gone off with him, a-flinging

    Leaving behind a spectral ringing

    Just like a wedding band -

For some these words are stinging

    But it's news of joy I'm bringing

    To girls like me a-wringing

    Wondering if they'll find their man.

With no human word, he tasted my lips,

    My guilt in gold clouds dissolving;

    No earthy fruit surpasses this –

    And I cupped his mouth in love's resolving.

King of Strangers in morning dreaming,

Riding high in his hidden garden -

Dragonfly of unseemly gleaming,

Taking harvest without care or pardon.

As a violin dances, he lifted us high

And I sought the God I'd looked for;

But love's true nature was searing my eye,

And I learned to thank the Goddess more.

For some the words are stinging

But it's news of joy I'm bringing,

To girls like me a-wringing

Wondering if they'll find their man --

Words they're always stringing,

    But have faith, he'll come a-winging

    Like me, you'll come a-singing

    With the starlight on your hand.

Elven eyes, elven eyes, I've seen without lies;

    Heard songs enchanted for ears sore -

    Runic rhymes drawing down the very skies,

    Once known, you canna ignore.

In forested halls of deathless depth

    I'll join him festively, and keen.

    I'll dwell eternally in his deathless death,

    Well-wrapped in leaves of green.

The Scarlet Maid and The Green Man

Her skin is fair, but
her hair is red-scarlet.
Don't go near her
today, or tonight

you'll pay

the price of a meeting with the forest harlot --

Red berries that sicken, nettles that snare,
Stinging bees that quicken the air near spider webs
that warn the traveller beware --

Tis better

to make friends with these

than

touch

even one

strand

of the Scarlet Maid's hair.

Wild and willful in the days

of old,

she ran through the forests

sun dappled green gold;

She couldn't be held to any

one spot

in her search for human flesh

to red and to rot.

Naked she ran through the greens,

Her body slender and white;

Her red mouth bit hard,

and that bite bit hardest at night.

She had a touch that would

stain a man's skin

So that no other woman

would hold him again.

Yet for all that, she had a place --

For she protected the forest

with her wild red grace.

One eve as she lay stretched at her ease,

the light cast a peculiar green through

the leaves --

In just that moment before sleep fell on her

her eyes flew open -- she felt other eyes upon her!

She turned and saw a magnificent man ahead,

Green moss fell in waves

from the Crown of his head,

The contours of his form were supple and tight,

His presence was strong

but his movements were light,

Swiftly he came towards her, she rose in flight --

but the Scarlet Maid was beguiled

by the Green Man that night.

She was no easy conquest –
she fought and she clawed,

but the Green Man was
patient,
and she became awed
as he held her with
strength, but tenderly,
and her bites turned into
caresses, eventually.

And so it was that the
Scarlet Maid was tamed,
and for her 'twas that
Poison Oak is named.

The Green Man still holds her wild nature dear,

Giving her his own sacred tree, the Oak, to live near.

She decorates the tree as her own home now,

twining her slender white body

'long the strong Oak bough,

Spreading the tresses of her carmen

hair, the Oak wears her colors,

warning travellers – take care!

As long as she still accepts this

home, and no longer over the forest

does roam, the forest is for us a

friendlier place --

Though she still does protect it

with her wild red grace.

Balalaika Song

Without a word the player strums his songs

Of lighter loves and deeper wrongs,

His hair falls in a black cascade,

His brows are black wings, blacker made

By his glance from under his turbaned hat,

And his heart casts a shadow blacker than that~~~

His handsome smile rarely gleams

Like when the dancer takes the stage

of his nighttime dreams,

She gives men hopes of foreign embraces

While the women wonder

How she earned those graces~~

Without a word she dances his songs
Of lighter loves and deeper
wrongs,
Many a woman has he taken
to bed,
But only this dancer has he
wished to wed~~

His balalaika balalaika
balalaika plays
Reminding him of other
women, other days,
The young girl dances in the
ancient ways
As his balalaika balalaika
plays!

Through her hennaed hair snakes silver coins,

Scarves and chains thread through her loins,

Onyx anklets and brass hand bells,

But only one ring which he knows so well;

From his father's father, of mixed ambers

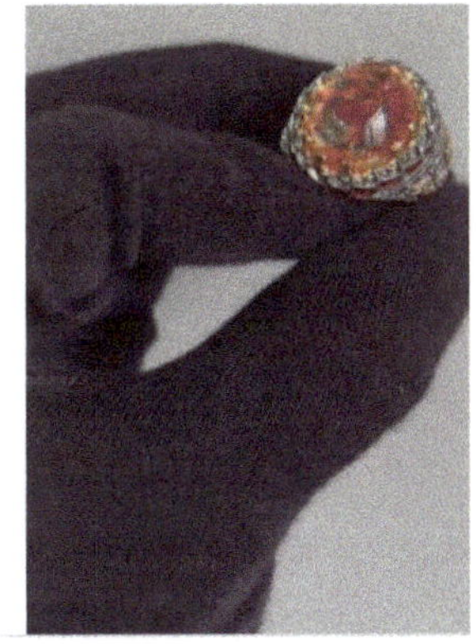 One dark midnight it became hers~~

The dancer's glance has

the dust of the desert,

Her gold dusted body the musk of the earth,

Her painted feet stamp the earth with a sigh,

Hips and hands sway the glance of her eye;

Through her hennaed hair snakes silver coins,

Scarves and chains thread through her loins,

But his dark glance on her hand now lingers,

His Ring is gone from the dancer's fingers!

His balalaika balalaika balalaika plays

Reminding him of other women, other days!

The young girl dances in the ancient ways

As his balalaika balalaika plays!

The plate is passing, the crowd is pleased,

Children run while men take their ease,

As one man stays and strolls to the stage

Where the Player's expression fires in rage;

For the Northerner has a smile for his dancer

And the ring on his finger and a ready answer!

The plate is passing, the crowd is pleased,

Children run while men take their ease,

A woman screams, a groan is heard

The Player runs his sword

Through the man without a word.

No one moves

red blood glistens

The dancer turns

everyone listens

As she falls

with a dying moan

At the feet of the man

that made her his own.

And so was shed

innocent blood,

For she'd given nothing

to the Northerner of love ~

Early that morning she had

sold him the ring

To buy the Player a home

and pay for their wedding.

The player was dragged away and chained

And that very midnight he was hanged;

But in his last moments in his stony cell,

They let him play the song he knew so well~~

Throughout the prison, in echoing wails

Came a darkened vision of a girl in veils;

The player was dragged away and chained

And that very midnight he was hanged,

But for a moment his song hung in the air,

And the shadow of his love was dancing there~~~

His balalaika, balalaika, balalaika plays,

Reminding him of other women, other days.

The young girl dances in the ancient ways

As his balalaika, balalaika plays…

Fish Child's Favorite

Under the Ocean floats an opulent hall

Where bubbly columns rise in pearly pall

Over sea grass pirouetting soundlessly

In a marvelous maritime symphony

In shallows nearby there's a wee nursery

Where golden sand sparkles the straw colored sea

Fish Child and sea fairies glimmeringly play

As far wiser creatures watch gently their way

Now down down deep

where Fish Child can't go

Green sea clouds release deep blue sea snow

Over Octopi waltzing through a Three Ring Show

With Baby Clams clapping in a tiny tango!

The Band Master wears

his best silver scales

Directing a chorus of

Blessed White Whales

Fierce orange Starfish

are twirling away

In their lovely and silent

underwater ballet…

Then! amid the millions of gurgling cheers

And more than an ocean of adoring salt tears…

A watery spotlight
captivates above!
The Seahorse Siren -
ssssinging of
ssSea Love…

Ohhhhhhhh

Ohhhhhhhhhhh
Ooooooooooooo
Aaaaaaaaaaaaa
Eeeeeeeaaaaaa
oooohhhhhhhhh
Mmuuuummmmmmmmmmmmmmmmm…..

And the whole house now is up in a roar!

While tossed on the surface, the sailors implore

To all the gods, but mostly Neptune

Oh please! Let the splendid sea concert end soon!

But no such prayer moves the King of the Deep

While enchanted silent calls from the Siren still

seep………..

While every Sea

Urchin, Sea

Lord and Sea

Maid

Dips, and

spellbound, is

timelessly

swayed…

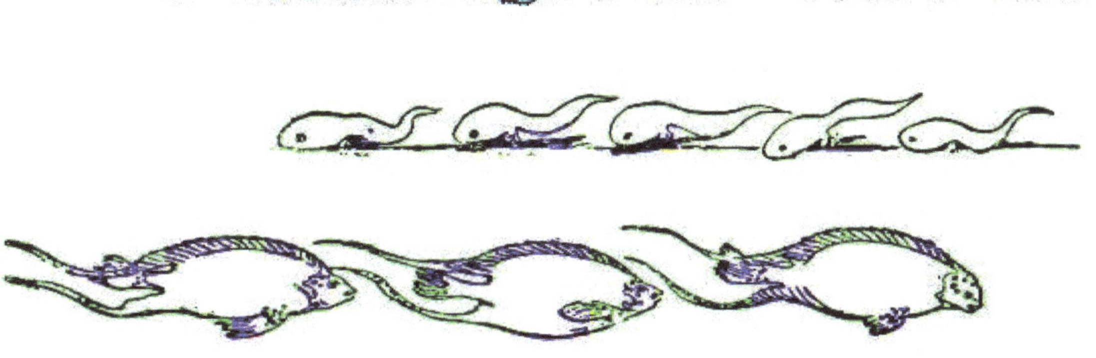

The Dolphin who Came Late

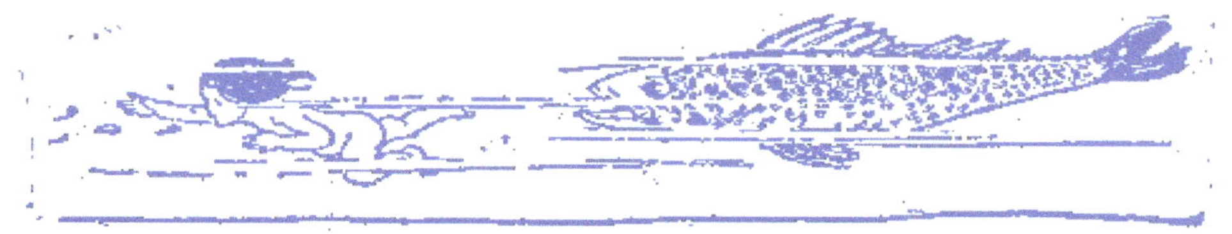

But even lovely things must come to an end,

And eventually they all went home for a swim,

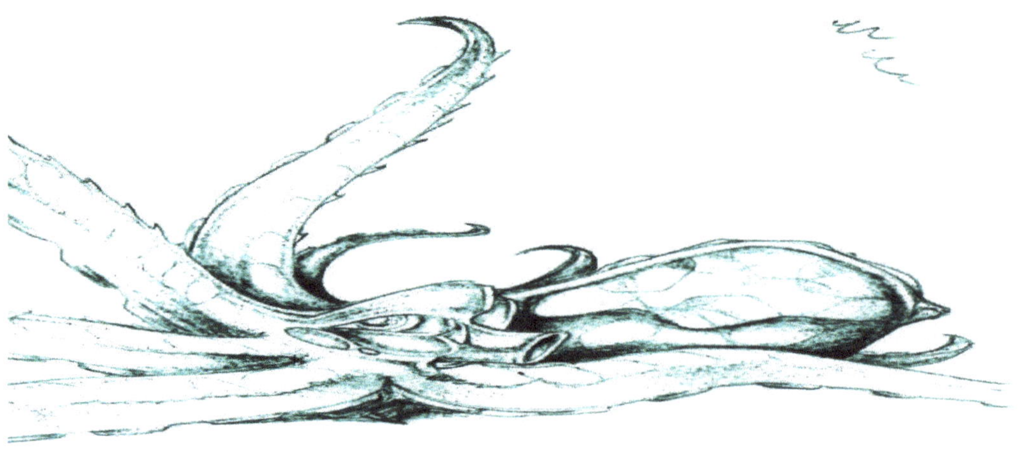

Rippling with laughter and fish tales

of glory –

That soon became Fish Child's

Best bedtime story.

AUTUMN

Time Thieves

Some steal a bit of the future
to live in an ordered present;
Some steal bits of the past
so futures may be more pleasant

Vanishing Muse

My Muse never lived with me

So I can't truly say,

Lifted by my searching heart

High and low,

One day she flew away

She is always ever free

And draws her life in Spring

From new made streams and

Roots and buds…

…

And every faery thing…

In autumn she is showering down

Along the roadway side

Or finding seed heads

Ripe to burst

On which she takes a ride

Wintertide she feeds the birds

With poetry of old,

Crafted by the fireside

Cast in spells

Of moonlight clear and cold

Summer is her true abode

Aside the sighing sea

Offering fruits and flowers,

Love's pure song,

She tries to comfort me

Invocation of Fall

Red auld wine, an

offering seeps through the

toes of this old tree.

High underneath these empty

branches

is better to be when people

come round like the bees

Every

one

senses

a tremblin' even though

its so below the surface…

Something old is stirred

     moved shaken awakened

     growling low slumbering

     rumblin lumberin

     moving while the earth

     is turning Still

       on its old illimitless course ~

This place takes us back to Ire land

    foggy dream and

    fairly fairy land

Hinter

hie,

Winter

nigh

It's harvest time and

we all die

The land is cold, we grow old

and night's nearby --

Gather round the family frown

    more comforting than sacred ground ~

Minutes pass ~ the earth turns

    Slower

    Colours deepen, Voices lower…

Leaves only rattle on

    Autumn's breath...

Red auld wine, an

    offering seeps through

    the toes of this olde tree

As far as it reaches no one breaches

the shadow

    it throws like a warm

    cloak for you,

    the seasonal traveller.

91

Rarebit

Quicksilver was her wit
Silver footed she used to
flit
In moonlight all night
long
Singing in a silver tongue,
Faceless o'er mirrored
pond,
No bent leaf or broken
frond -
So lightly she made her way,
The girl who was a fae.

Shimmers shaped o'er the lake
But the visions didn't take
Instead she'd wiggle her ears
To hear what a tree root hears,

Spiders gaining her friendship,
Field mice earning her kinship -
Keeping quiet counsel by day,
The girl who was a fae.

She combed
her hair in
fingers
Finding where
the sweet air
lingers,
Warmed by the
honey bee
As real as
you or me,

Wheat catching on a hair strand,
A thorn even scratching her hand –

There a drop of blue blood lay,

From the girl who was a fae.

As a child is airy and mild,

As a sylph is winsome

and wild,

Both streaks sparked

through her blood

High elf mingling

human mud,

Her earthen tread too

light,

Though not wholly of

the night -

Neither fair chance had

they,

In this girl who was a fae.

Fullsome fall fell afire -

She took an apple basket entire

All on a faery dare

Childish one, without a care;

While a barren young Lady-wife
Spied her and hoped to save a life -
Foolish, to take home a stray
Like the girl who was a fae.

Nearby strode the Gamekeeper
Out today to find the creeper,
That thief who made the apple run
Hard on its course
and under his gun!

Two different hearts set for a prize
Seeing each other with fair surprise -
From opposite sides closed they,
On the girl who was a fae.

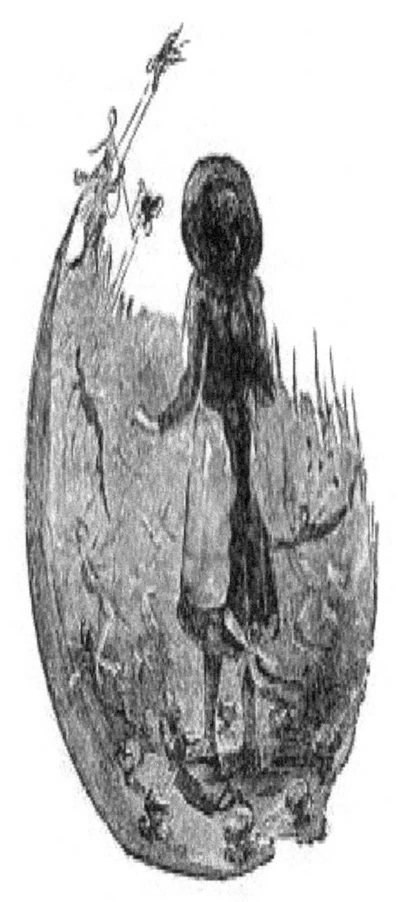

To a man's hunt he was bound

With or without the lazy hound

Heading into the clearing fast

Weapon raised and ready to blast!

To pause isn't the hunter's game,

Creature or thief's tail all the same --

In the clearing there she lay,

The girl who was a fae.

And on that silenced

hallowed ground

The Lady-wife wept

without a sound

Her face a tracked and pallid peak

Her child of a moment never to speak ~~

As

before their god-fearing souls,

Dead eyes rolling back in their holes -

There only a silver hare lay,

The girl who was a fae.

Every time a
new story is told
a fairy is born

To Wee Russet Tuft

Your wee, adorable heart is stilled

In your small sweet feathered breast,

Still warm from the life within it plucked

Just now from its dear, warm nest.

Your tiny green head curved so neat,

Your pearly neck so prettily puffed,

And atop your lovely, delicate brow

You sported your little russet tuft.

More innocent even than a babe

Who at least cries, you had no other thought

Than to adorn branches like a gem

And sing what the morning sun had brought.

Your mother laboured so to feed you,

Taught you the tricks and the bliss of flight;

Does she know your button eyes have closed

On the dark of Death's eternal night?

It is my deep wish little Russet Tuft
That when Death found you, it was swift -
You never knew what evil took you,
So Fear could miss that graveyard shift.

It is my deeper hope
little one,
You did not die in pain
for all that,

You left somehow
before the Devil
pounced,
Enrobed in her velvet
jacket of Cat.

She is being punished, of course.

Jailed all this day that seems too long -

But there is no real way to seek recourse

For your stainless soul who did no wrong.

Your death is on my hands as well;

I harbor the Devil and give her my love.

She gives in to mere animal nature,

While I know full well what she's capable of.

Wild wee Russet Tuft,

I'm sad to say

In a poem your short

life lives on;

Your bright chirping is now exchanged

For this sweet but sad and tuneless song.

107

Onyx

She knows no gratitude,

Nor mercy, nor pain;

Dainty demonette

Demanding only respectful

Devotion, now and again.

Needling nails and teeth

Continuously red;

Luminous gemstone coat

Cloaking masquerade glances,

And dances with the dead.

From realms of avian hells,

Sinister jonglette;

Leaping to death knells

Ringing from her

Jingling collar bells!

Murderess' heart under

Pure green eyes divine;

Patroness of driest caresses

When I rarely please

That cat of mine.

"THE BODY OF THE WHITE CAT GREW LARGE AND WAS TRANSFORMED INTO THAT OF A GIRL."

The Spice Box

The little room I dream in

Is a Keep unto myself;

Sitting high amid the trees,

A vaulted chamber in sepia lees,

A world set apart on soft seas

Bygone of pain and worry.

It is a box of valued spices

Kept on a golden shelf

By a calm mistress whose device is

A poetic key upon her belt -

Whilst inside amongst the fairy

Perfumes, I am the curry.

And open now, the
blinds just so,
To sparkling fishes
on the breeze;

Distant children's happy shouts

Pouring through, and colors too;

Like the crystal

invites the

rainbow

Through

realms

unknown to

hurry.

Djer-Kiss Talc
—the warm summer through

Made in Paris, Djer-Kiss Talc brings to you quite l'air exquis, a fascination so quite Parisian. And what a softness and purity—what a fragrance of refinement! With what smoothness after le bain! With what a soothingness in warm weather!

Surely, Mademoiselle, more than ever you will love this unusual French Talc—Djer-Kiss Talc—the warm summer through.

Djer-Kiss
"Made in France"

EXTRACT • FACE POWDER • TALC • SACHET
TOILET WATER • VEGETALE • SOAP

In return for fifteen cents
the Alfred H. Smith Company, 40 West 34th St., New York City, will be happy to send you samples of Djer-Kiss Extract, Face Powder and Sachet.

WINTER

Pale sun burnishing pale gold -
Warming legendary tales gone cold,
Calling forth her fireside heroes;
The Queen Fae chants stories of old…

Dreamtime

Magician on one leg, Black Bird
So poised, so poised
In the biting white wind
Belonging between all the noise

How do you do that Black Bird?
How do you turn into
The Face of Nature
yet stay so still

Teaching the lesson of Strength of Will.

Mage of balance, Black Bird
Leg in the air on a fence
Watching, seeing everywhere
Through the eye of the wild elements
Alert yet perfectly still,
Teaching the lessons of Strength of Will,

Living the lesson of Strength of Will.

Helland

In Scotland now

The bitter winds die down,

A dead souls journey

beneath the surface of

the still earth

The bitter winds die down,

Down,

through the openings of caves where

the last sunlight plays

at the backs of people like children peering,

Peering,

into the darkness

of that other cold

world so nearing...

Down and

down

echo

the earth's

sounds,

Through tree roots

remote and

fields of stones

underground,

Cut by black rivers

flaring in the glare of

hot metal waterfalls,

Fiery waterfalls!

running through

endless processions

of rock chambers

opening

Into enormous kingly halls of

jutting purple amethyst and white crystals glistening,

Glistening --

in the green glow of a subterranean lake;

Here my ancient bridegrooms

sit listening,

Listening --

On giant iron thrones

Making signs to

one another

to relinquish to

my mother

and my mother's mother

The Crone

The old oaths that hold me.

Three kings in glinting metal crowned are weeping

diamonds unaware that their

hard expressions are no less

sincere

than the tenderest woman's

womans' tear.

Each hand forged crown bears

a crystal gem of power, it's

color, like a lantern light

streaming

where its wearer

chooses to turn his head

Lighting the dominions

of these earth bound men

with the energy

of blue, green and red.

The ruler of all underground waters

The ruler of all life passing from below to above

The ruler of all underground fires

learned long ago that united

In the Earth's virgin love

Their community of three

became

the

world's

mighty

male

trinity.

Here were drafted ancient workings of antiquity,

Gold was spun into sandals to bind

the feet of a flighty deity;

Warrior's armor, like fine silk was conceived,

and those delicate chains

which entice a woman to

link her neck, nose, waist

and ear, forever

binding herself

to the house of one

who holds her too dear.

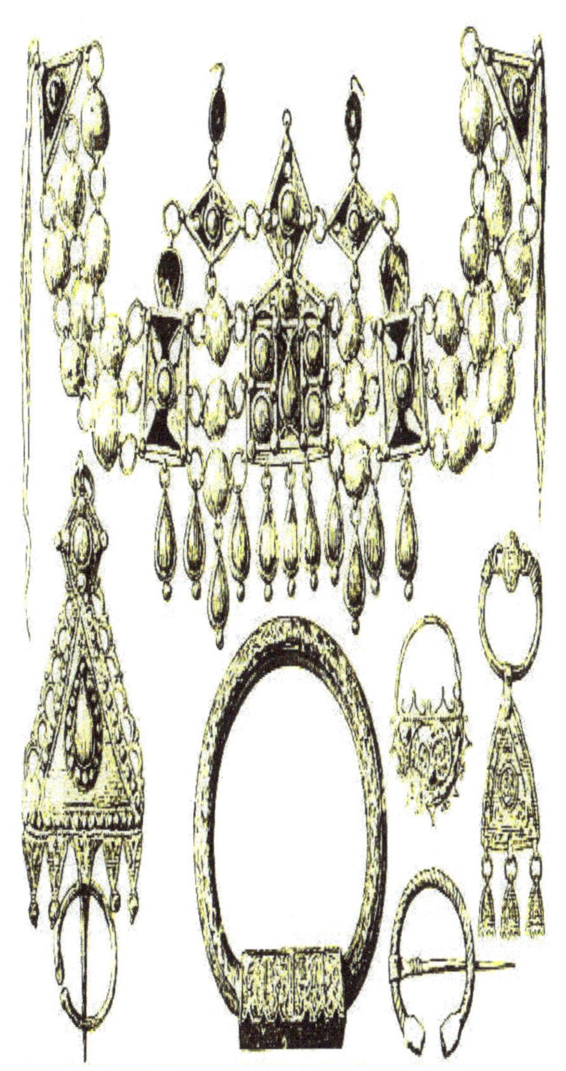

And on and on the

storehouses grew,

Piled with rarities

rough and fine

which only the

armies of these

artistic miners knew

how to make and

where to find;

And on and on the

storehouses grew

as the earth revealed her treasures to her three loves

Who nightly she whispered her secrets to.

*** *** ***

Once I sat so

cold and alone

and from the seat of

my silver throne

hammered with care

to trap me where

I call out in despair;

From my magnificent

silver throne I call out

to my mother and my

mother's mother

the Crone.

My bridegrooms' works are all around me

To amuse and surround me with memories

from far above, Painstakingly crafted with the forged

love of metal smithies~

Crystal clocks chiming

underground to count the

countless

hours timing…

Birds formed of brilliant

glass rhyming

false tunes through subtle

mechanical wiring.

Sapphires and garnets

too heavy to wear,

Nets of diamonds and

opals to catch my hair,

Even a false moon and

stars tricked from Mercury

Are hung there where

real ones would be…

My dress is of metal cloth

spun from three colors of

gold, like everything,

Everything here

brittle, metallic and cold.

Spirit of the

Windward Isle

The wind is a way-weary

mistress

Whose breeze curries

sailors to sea;

She laughs in their ears

in a tempest

And cries through their eyes to be free.

But she rocks and she calms all the babies

In small houses on the sea, by the shore -

Then she takes the salt tears of the ladies

And cries them once more.

It was here that I grew into youth,

The sounds of the waves in my hair;

Just briefly the sunshine could soothe

Our haunted blue shores of despair.

The shadows will talk to young

sailors

In shanties of madness

that passes --

But then come the blue

tears of whalers,

And the black tales of lasses.

They say Hell is a flaming

damnation

And the Devil knows every

last sin,

But they know no blue hell

like my nation

With its thousand tears

sown by the wind.

Now I wend from black depths to above,

I've no peace in my old haunt the sea -

The wind has become my one love

And the phantom of me.

The Baallad of Blaackie Coal

Wance upon a time, lang time ago

Nothing was explained we didnae know,

But these days lack alla mystery

So this couldnae happened -

Though the witness is me.

The year wis fast into last quarter rind,

The field lambs left a' milkin' behind

When white Mary Ewe cut the deep content

   With her birthing bellow of - Baa baa baa!

Like a mirky lament.

CHORUS:

Ol' Clootie musta gotten luckie

Or mibbie 'twas Goodfellow Puckie

Or th'De'il himself who found a way

Over sweet Mary Ewe afore Yuletide day

He didnae ken howcome he's here

He didnae ken aboot a soul,

Didnae ken why Mary licked him clean,

And he was still as black as coal.

Neither flock nor ram took a blade o' joy

In the little black shadow deemed Satan's boy,

Could barely see him if he drew near

Calling out his friendly - baa baa baa!

Made them leap from Blaackie 'n his Dam so dear.

Like an Ugly Duckling without

any friends

He pursued his betters to make amends;

But they'd all shiver 'n' bolt for th' clover

     With their cowardly bleating - baa!baa! baaaaa

-Leavin' lil Blaackie a wee lonely rover.

CHORUS:

Auld Hornie musta bin in luck

Or mibbie 'twas Greenman Puck

Or th' De'il 'imself did fun a way

To visit Mary Ewe afore Christmas Day

He didnae ken howcome he's here,

He didnae ken aboot his soul,

Didnae ken why they're so hard on him

Callin' him Blaackie Coal.

Like Rudolph the Red-Nosed deer

He just wanted games and good cheer!

But the herd would turn and hightail away

   Crying out alarms of – Baa! Baaa!! Baaaa!!!

'cause he was born black on Christmas Day.

Dame Mary paid the fools no mind,

Loved little Blackie 'n' milked him fine,

Showin' him howfur to kick up his heels

   With her skylarking song o' - Ba baa baa!

While th' biggest ram turns trots 'n' squeals!

141

CHORUS:

Auld Nickie musta bin up in luck

  Or mibbie 'twas Good Faerie Puck

Or th' De'il 'imself who had his way

  with miss Mary Ewe afore Yuletide day

He didnae ken howfur he's here

He didnae ken aboot his soul,

He didnae ken how he put afear n them

  Cursin 'im as Blaackie Coal.

Blackie 'n' his dam walked a country lane

Found a black sheep croft in County Caine;

Were welcomed without a shred o' shame

    Flock singin like a choir -Baaaa Baaa baaaaaa

And like a prince o' peace now he does reign.

This all happen' a short time ago,

I ken ye don't believe, but 'twas truly so.

So today there *still* may be some mystery,

    We ken wi' a loud happy – Baa, Baa, Baaa!

And the witness is me.

CHORUS:

Auld Clootie musta bin up in luck

Or mibbie 'twas sir Brownie Puck

Or the De'il 'imself that fun a way

To sweet Mary Ewe afore Christmas Day

Now he *does* ken howfur he's here -

He kens he has a good fine soul,

Still canna ken why some are silly 'boot him,

'Cause he's just auld Blaackie Coal.

Fairy-Beauty rocks a Babe.

The Dream Fairy

A Bedtime Poem

In my Chamomile Cottage

Down the river Slipstream,

Under the Land of Nod

In the country of Dream -

I awake most evenings

From my long daydream nap

To milk the honeybees

In my spiderweb cap.

I fluff the moon's pillows,

Inspect all the stars' lights

Sing lullabies to the trees,

And wind the Clock Of Nights.

I feed the stray dust bunnies

Under my bedclothes of blue;

Set up my watch-candle, and

Start imagining all of you.

THE SURPRISE

Thus begins the artful craft

Of spinning forth your dreams

Out of glow worm threads

Lacing up firefly beams!

In Mother-of-Pearl tints

Netting puffs of starlight,

Here and there a soft feather

Or coloured gem beaming bright.

I fold Time Unto Itself --

Guide lost memories home,

Taking all sleepy children

On their long nightly roam.

Each mantle of dreams

Is newly woven again,

So every night it seems

Days deeds may unspin...

All wilding adventures

Are yours for the taking-

Flying and exploring

Thought-worlds of your making.

We'll weave it all together,

You and I in the dark,

'Til rosy Dawn sets her finger

On my watch-candle mark.

When the sun finally leaps

Through my window at morn,

I lay down night's works

To welcome Day Newborn.

I retire to my reveries

With a nightcap of strong dew,

Gathering new bundles of wonders

You'll soon be dreaming too!

158

" And, sweetly singing round about thy bed,
Strew all their blessings on thy sleeping head."

Far Rockaway

A Lullaby

The treetops are Gumdrops

And the raindrops are

Lollipops

In the town of

Far Rock-Away

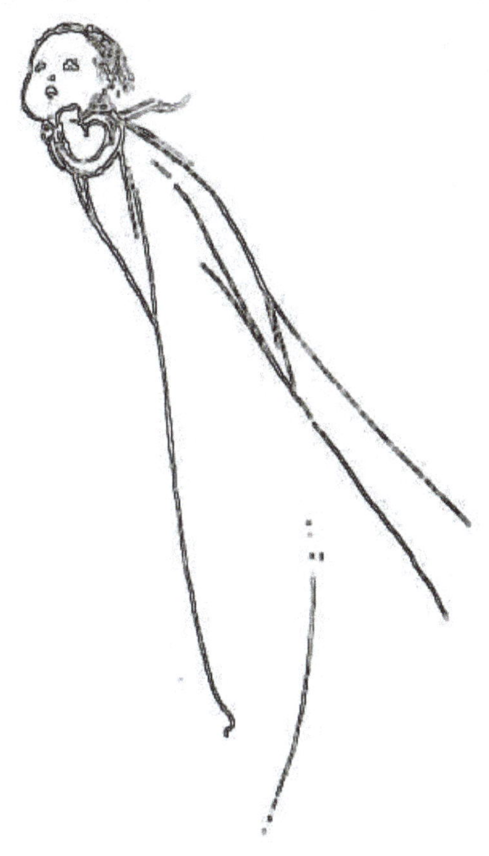

Where Marshmallow Rivers

Run by Graham Cracker Houses

And a Chocolate Cat

Licks on Liquorice Mouses

In the town

of Far Rock-Away

Where a little girl dreams

Of Giant Toffee Crèmes

And a little boy prays

For Double Holidays

They ask us to come and Please Play~

Riding the sky

lit by Custard Moon

Pie,

In our Ice Cream

Boat rounding

the Caramel Moat,

They invite us to

come now and

Play....

We'll find friends

in Far Rock-Away…

MAN or WOMAN
BOY or GIRL
THAT READS WHAT
FOLLOWS
3 TIMES
SHALL FALL ASLEEP
AN HUNDRED YEARS
JOHN D BATTEN DREW THIS : AUG 30th 1891
GOOD·NIGHT

167

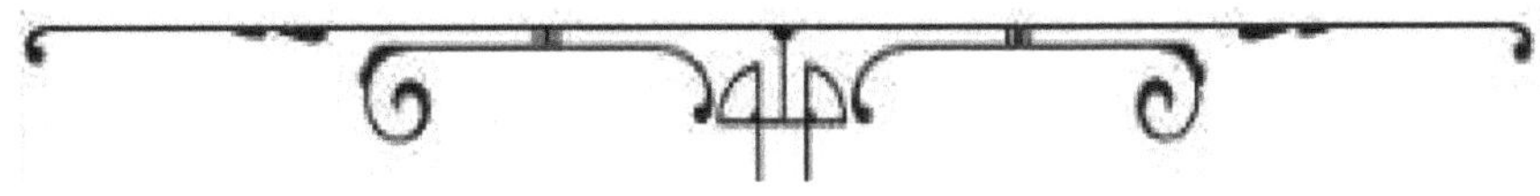

TABLE OF ILLUSTRATIONS

Note: All possible care has been taken to credit the artists who created the illustrations used in Fairy Lights. Please send any corrections to the author.

Page, Artist, *Name of Work, Publication* **(Author), [Medium]**if known, **Date**

ILLUSTRATIONS, cont'd

ILLUSTRATIONS, cont'd

70. Henry Justice Ford, *The Orange Fairy Book (*Lang), 1906
70. Dugald Stewart Walker, *Rainbow Gold* (Teasdale), 1922
71. Franz Heinz, *Nymph and Goldfish*, [print], c.1900
72. Walter Crane, *The Faerie Queen (*George Allen), 1897
72. Linley Sambourne, *The Water-Babies (*Kingsley), 1885
73. John D. Batten, *Europa's Fairy Book* (Jacobs), 1916
73. Linley Sambourne, *The Water-Babies (*Kingsley), 1885
73. Tom from TomTom Crew, <u>Tom@bornfresh.com.au</u>, [ink on napkin], 2011
74. Linley Sambourne, *The Water-Babies* (Kingsley), 1885 (multiple)
75. Elsa Beskow, *Grandmother Mushroom*, 1923
76. Kenny Meadows, *Shakespeare's Twelfth Night* (Meadows), 1843
76. Ida Outhwaite, *Goodbye to Potty,* 1921
77. Helen Jacobs, *Little Folks* magazine, (Osborne), 1920
78. Dugald Stewart Walker, *Rainbow Gold* (Teasdale), 1897
79. Cicely Mary Barker, *Lord of the Rushie River,* 1938
80. Richard Doyle, *The Fairy Queen Takes An Airy Ride*, c.1870
81. Unknown, [free digital wallpaper]
82. Warwick Goble, *The Book of Fairy Poetry* (Owen), 1920 (modified)
83. Margaret Tarrant, *A Jolly Jig*, [Christmas card], 1920
84. Franklin Booth, *Autumn Leaves*, Collier's Nov. 25, 1911
85. Rene Cloke, *Fairies Sweeping Autumn Leaves* [Valentine #1328], 1920
86. Ida Rentoul Outhwaite, *Elves & Faires* (A. Rentoul), 1919
87. Margaret Tarrant, *The Orchard Fairies* (Webb), 1928
88. Richard Doyle, *Fairies on Lillypad*, [postcard] c.1870
89. Ida Rentoul Outhwaite, *Elves & Fairies* (A. Rentoul), 1919
90. Constance Cary, *The Old-fashioned Fairy Book*, 1884
91. H.J. Ford, *How the Fairies Came to See, The Red Romance Book*, 1921
92. Ida Rentoul Outhwaite, *The Enchanted Forest*, 1921
93. Don Daily, *The Velveteen Rabbit* (Williams), 1922
93. Katherine Pyle, *Mother's Nursery Tales,* 1918
94. Ida Rentoul Outhwaite, *Spider Orchid*, 1933
95. Dorothy Wheeler, *The Dragonfly*, c. 1920s
96. Ida Rentoul Outhwaite, *The Enchanted Forest*, 1921
97. Florence Harrison, *The Elfin Song*, 1912
97. Rabbit, [free clip art silhouette]

ILLUSTRATIONS, cont'd

ILLUSTRATIONS, cont'd

136. Jenny Harbour, *My Book of Favorite Fairy Tales* (Vredenberg), 1921
137. *German Bestiary*, courtesy of New York Public Library, c.1805
138. Unknown, *Greek Faun* [tattoo art]
139. Unknown, *Mother Goose*, antique
140. Unknown, *Brownie* [drawing], 19th century
140. Unknown, *Krampus* [postcard], 19th century
142. Jacques Henri E. De Seve, *Histoire Naturelle* (Buffon), c.1788
144. Blanche Fisher Wright, *The Real Mother Goose*, 1910
146. Winslow Pinney Pels, *Lambscape* [color pencil drawing], vintage
147. Ida R. Outhwaite, Fairy beauty rocks a babe, *The Enchanted Forest,* 1921
150. Hilda Cowham, *The Surprise*, 1923
151. Harry Theaker, *Water Babies* (Kinglsey), 1930
154. Marguerite Davis, End of a Child's Day, *Field Fourth Reader* (Field), 1925
155. George Soper, *Tales From Shakespeare* (Lamb), 1909
158. Margaret Tarrant, The Babes in the Woods, *Fairy Tales*, c. 1920
159. Warwick Goble, *Book of Fairy Poetry* (Owen), 1920
160. Lolli, [free clip art]
160. Chas Robinson, *Lilliput Lyrics* (Johnson), [sheet music], 1899
161. Composite image, clockwise top: Blanche Fisher Wright *Peter Patter Book* (Jackson), 1918; Hildegard Lupprian, *Honey Land*, 1927; Cat [free clip art]
162. Ekaterina Vitchenko, Toffee [free clip art] (modified)
163. Hilda T. Miller, *The Rose Fyleman Fairy Book* (Fyleman), 1923
164. Blanche Fischer Wright, *Peter Patter Book* (Jackson), 1918 (modified)
165. Clara M. Burd, *Good Stories for Great Holidays* (Olcott), 1914
166. Jessie Wilcox Smith, *The Little Mother Goose*, 1912
166. Jessie Wilcox Smith, *The Little Mother Goose*, 1912
166. John Dixon Batten, *More Celtic Fairy Tales* (Jacobs), 1891
167. Maginel Wright Enright, *Flower Fairies* (Judson), 1915
177. Edmund H. Garrett, *Brownies and Bogles* (Guiney), 1888
178. Katharine Pyle, *Mother's Nursery Tales*, 1918

Note: Where an illustration came with a caption, I included it; Art Nouveau page decorations are from free digital collections.

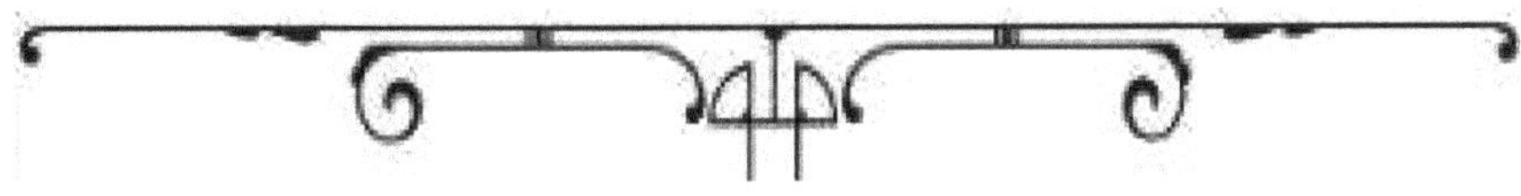

FRONT COVER

Midsummer's Eve By

Edward Robert Hughes, watercolor, 1908.

Hughes' self portrait

E.R. Hughes, known by family as "Ted" (5 November 1851 – 23 April 1914) was a British painter known for his fantastically beautiful watercolours, a number of oil paintings, and his early portraits of the upper classes. He was influenced by his uncle and artist Arthur Hughes who was associated with the Pre-Raphaelite Brotherhood, and worked closely with one of the Brotherhood's founders, William H. Hunt.

Hughes held several important offices within the artistic community over his lifetime, and was a committee member of the Art Workers Guild. He was elected to the Royal Watercolour Society (ARWS) in1891, and he chose as his diploma work a mystical piece *Oh, What's That in the Hollow?*. A painting of his was chosen by the RWS to be gifted to King Edward VII and Queen Alexandra to mark their coronation in 1902.

Ted Hughes served as a studio assistant to Pre-Raphaelite W.H. Hunt and provided a great deal of assistance on some of Hunt's finest works during his latter years as his vision declined. Two of the paintings they produced *were The Light of the World*, which is displayed in St Paul's Cathedral, and *The Lady of Shalott*, which is exhibited at the Wadsworth Atheneum.

His works can be seen in public collections including Bradford, Cambridge & County Folk Museum, Maidstone Museum & Art Gallery, Bruce Castle Museum, Kensington Central Library, Birmingham Museum and Art Gallery, the Ashmolean at Oxford, the Harris Museum & Art Gallery, Preston, Cartwright Hall, and the National Trust for Scotland.

Birmingham Museums Trust staged a retrospective exhibition, "Enchanted Dreams: The Pre-Raphaelite Art of E.R. Hughes", in 2015 at Birmingham Museum and Art Gallery.

His auction record is $866,500 (£522,366) for *Dream Idyll (A Valkyrie*, sold at Sotheby's (New York) on 22 October 2009.

NOTES ON POEMS

12. Timegarden – written over several hours on a rainy day in Dunedin in a teacher's lounge at Otago University, that had wonderful huge tall windows like a conservatory.

14. St. Paddy's Fete – after a long slough of no poetry writing, I was struck and inspired by the John Anster Fitzgerald painting, "Rabbit Among Fairies". It was St. Patrick's Day, hence the name.

21. A Piece of Amber – an illustration of Fae lore and how fairies mate and marry. Notice that everything in the fairy world is upside-down – the feminine spirit is solar, the masculine is lunar. It also recalls the Heliades - sisters of the sun who wept amber at the death of their brother Phaeton. When I wrote this I echoed the rhyming lines of a poem about knights and their ladies fair, but I never could find the poem I was haunted by. The first lines of the repeated chorus mimic the lightly running sounds of a stream.

29. The Redeemables – this poem has a depth I did not discover until later. Always a sunrise Easter poem, I found that the Irish Brigid was a persona that had morphed over time from a legendary Queen of the Fae to a beloved Catholic Saint. Thus it seemed to me that she and her fae troops were redeemable from their heathen ways which they partially retained, while welcomed into the church in the eyes of Christ and the host of Saints. And it is a fun romp close to the fae as they troop at night, singing!

33. My Monumental Teeth - what if we became suddenly smaller even than Alice in Wonderland? Or we noticed parts of ourselves seemed unaccountably big, like in an uncanny dream?

37. My Waikouaiti Lass – I was excited to be moving to the North Island, yet felt guilty over leaving my Waikouaiti home, after the beautiful land had been so sweet and good. The influence was the wooing poems and love affairs of Robert Burns, who I studied closely to enter and win the Dunedin Burns Society poetry contest, seat of the most active Burns Society in the world at present.

41. The Elder Tree – woke up and wrote this down in about 30 minutes, while my husband was showering. Envision the narrator as an old blind woman in a marketplace, somewhere in the Nordic lands. Every day she repeats this tale, sometimes mocked, sometimes earning a few coins. Is she mad, or did this really happen to her? Was she unwanted, rejected and abused, until she found solace in this affair in which she was given a gleaming star-like engagement ring on her finger? When I wrote this, I was not aware that in Nordic lore, falling asleep under certain trees could cause encounters with magical beings which could grant favors or madness; even abductions, marriages and eternal life.

49. The Scarlet Maid and the Green Man - a rare North American myth based on the ancient Greek or Roman style of explaining natural phenomenon with stories of gods and nature beings, such as the myths of Narcissus, Echo, Apollo and Daphne, and Persephone's marriage to Pluto. Poison Oak, or *Toxicodendron diversilobum*, mimics the shape of the oak leaf and grows as a shrub or vine near or in oak trees and habitat. It is green until autumn, when its leaves turn scarlet. The Oak has long been associated with the Green Man, the masculine side of the natural world.

59. Balalaika Song – listen to how he plays the balalaika in the choruses- normal, angry, deeply sad. The balalaika repetition mimics the guitar-like sound of the instrument. Inspired by the mysterious dancers of the Gypsy Bellydance Stage at the fabled and fabulous Renaissance Faire in southern California, I opened some of their performances with this poem, costumed as a wandering bard.

65. Fish Child's Favorite – one day wading in shallow waves of Waikouaiti bay, I felt little fish nibbling my toes! This was so delightful I began looking for them through the clear waves and wheat colored underwater sand, which sparkled gold in the sunshine. This seemed to be a nursery for the wee ones, and everything flowed from there.

78. Vanishing Muse – in my view, the Muse can never really be captured and cannot be imprisoned without losing its essential nature. If we are lucky, we may sketch a glimpse of our inspiration or contain a moment of it behind the glass walls of verse or in a painting or song. Bn truth, it is an ongoing, living relationship of highs and lows.

83. Invocation of Fall – the first poem I wrote during my fateful "Night At Greystone" described in an essay in my book *Chimera*. There was a time when it seemed that autumn would not come in LA until I finally spoke this poem aloud, which would break the late summer spell. "Leaves only rattle on Autumn's breath" is a phrase I swear I knew in my childhood, but I've never found the poem.

92. Rarebit – one day my fiancé Philip and I walked in an old California live oak grove, and the sunshine warmed the long wheat and tall grasses, which exuded a sweet perfume, like honey. The next morning after waking I wrote Rarebit down all in a session of about a half hour or so. I'm not sure of the connection but the walk and the fragrance definitely inspired the poem. Baudelaire's "Une Chargone" (A Carcass) played a role as well.   Rarebit is a Welsh dish of cheese and toast that is a wry joke on

175

not having rabbit to eat if the hunt was poor. My fae Rarebit stands for the inherent natural and elemental nature of both the land and of children, too often laid to waste by the civilizing impulses represented by The Huntsman and The Lady-wife.

103. To Wee Russet Tuft – winner of the Burns Society poetry contest in Dunedin. This event really happened, and the tiny bird brought in by Onyx expired while cradled in my hands, even as its bright coloring seemed timelessly cheerful. It was New Year's Day, and I felt so bereft, I vowed this anonymous little bird's loss of life would not be in vain, and at least would be mourned in writing. Robert Burns wrote a few poems to humble small animals, highlighting their innocence and often unfair conditions in life living near or with mankind.

108. Onyx - cats are fascinating, contrarian, and mysterious, inspiring a genre of poetry all their own, and a considerable online presence as well. The pride of any household, they reside in elevated climes of our hearts. Many poets have written of them, but my favorite *fête des félins* is Baudelaire's "Le Chat. Write your poem about a feline today!.

111. The Spice Box – can a little room of one's own become an escape to Arcadia, Shangri-la or Shambala? When one finally finds peace and quiet and can indulge in daydreams lit by motes of sunshine, a room becomes a haven and a heaven.

117. Dreamtime – this really happened, as I was in my spice box room during a heavy storm, I looked out my window and saw a large black corvid standing on one leg very close by facing a raging wind, rain and thunder. How could he stand there for hours and never even once put his foot down?   When animals present so forcefully it is good to pay attention and consider the message, as from a sage.

119. Helland – written on Mother's Day of that year, there is something ancient here about agreements for good or ill between women of different generations, represented by the Triple Goddess. Persephone and earthy elementals known as Dwarves appear. The Underground, technology, automatons, and the earth's energies are mysteriously fused in a seemingly timeless dimension of capture, surrender, and endurance.

131. Spirit of the Windward Isle – a rare species of poem – a collaboration. Written with my husband one relaxed afternoon on our deck. He wrote a line, then I wrote one, and back and forth. I have no idea how this poignant and haunting output emerged from the two of us, because nothing like it was on our minds at all. This is the magic of poetry extracting itself in a sort of automatic operation from our souls. The poem's secret is that you don't really realize until the end that the narrator is a restless ghost. Boo!

137. The Baallad of Blaackie Coal –this story really happened in Waikouaiti on our property. A black-as-coal sheep was born from a white flock of ewes and gelded males on or very near Christmas day, well after lambing season. Where did he come from? Who sired him? As a wee little fella he frightened the heck out of the entire flock of rather hefty mature sheep, who ran away hilariously bleating whenever he came near, except his good mother. He and his dam were given to a black sheep breeder where he fit in and lived a happy life. At the time I was heavily enraptured of Burns, whose poetic tales of good God-fearing Scots with their bogies and folky names for the devil seemed the only way to tell this story. I hope Blaackie's "tail" will live on in loud and emotive baaa baa-baa-ing of children during story time and even bedtime. Counting sheep with eyes closed could follow.

148. The Dream Fairy – the poem that inspired me to collect *Fairy Lights* as a book of bedtime story-poems for children. Years after writing about her, as I put together this book I found she had often been illustrated in days past as often as the Fairy Queen and more than the Tooth Fairy. She's an icon of delight and safe passage through night time sleep and dreams. The Dream Fairy is hardly spoken of today, yet so vital to the imaginations of children and the inner child in all of us.

160. Far Rockaway – just a very simple lullaby lyric, written at the request of a friend for her wee baby nephew. When I was a kid, I read every page of an illustrated encyclopedia of children's poems, and *The Sugar Plum Tree* captured my imagination! The poet Eugene Field explains that you could only get the delectable candies hanging from the tree by making the gingerbread dog bark at the chocolate cat, who would run around the branches of the tree shaking the treats loose in wonderful and innocent mayhem! I had long forgotten these things when writing the lullaby, but found the poem again when writing these notes – at last, a case of an old verse lost to memory recovered! The Chocolate Cat lives on, much less stressed, in a faraway dream town of pleasure. When I was very small, I dreamed more than once of flying up through the ceiling to a sunlit attic where I played with a small girl like me and her very kind mother. Having a boat would have been icing on the cake, moon pie, toffee creams, long holidays, lollies, chocolate cat and even a squeaky liquorice mouse or two. Yum!

About the author, Helen Williford-Lower

I live in New Zealand with my physics teacher husband
Philip and two very funny cats - Nimbus 2000 who can run
with live butterflies in his mouth without harm, and formerly
feral Lady Jane Gray. Fairy Lights is published on April 9,
sharing the birthday of two of my favorite poets, Laurence
Hope and Charles Baudelaire.

Website: fairylightsbook.com

Contests:
1st Place Winner of the NZ Burns Society Poetry Contest, 2015
1st Place Winner of the Caselberg Trust Poetry Prize, 2025 and
         Featured in the 250th Edition of *Landfall Tauraka*

Previous Books:
Cameo
The Poisoned Cup
A Piece of Amber
Chimera
Chimère (édition Française)
The Magic Hour

Available on Amazon
and many online dealers

FAIRY STORIES.

Spoken Word::
Chimeras CD
India's Love Lyrics, by Laurence Hope - for Libravox

Blog: laurencehopenotes.blogspot.com

Contact: fairylightsbook@gmail.com

This book has no AI images or writing.